W9-ACV-105

DISCARD

Small Knight
∽ and the ∽
Anxiety Monster

Manka Kasha

Feiwel and Friends
New York

There once lived a knight.

The knight was very small,

but noble and brave,

as any real knight should be.

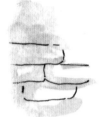

The king and queen hoped their child

would be a proper princess. But that wasn't

what Small Knight wanted at all!

"It's not that being a princess is bad,"

Small Knight complained to their best friend, Tiny Bear.

"It's just that I don't think it's for me.

I'd prefer going on adventures with you!"

But how to explain all that to their mom and dad?

Small Knight was so worried they'd be upset.

The worry kept growing day by day, during the

Proper Princess Lessons and crowded meetings.

It was hiding under the table during meals, and

under the bed at night, until . . .

One morning, Small Knight woke up to see a

huge, shadowy monster in their room.

Now, Small Knight was, indeed, very brave, but

something about this silent giant made them very scared.

The monster never spoke, but it followed Small Knight and

Tiny Bear everywhere—and no one else could see it!

"There's a huge monster following me,"

Small Knight said to their parents.

"Such a vivid imagination!" the king exclaimed.

"Don't worry, dear, you're very safe in your tower,

and even if there were a monster,

it's just a part of being a princess!

One day a brave knight will save you!"

"But I AM a brave knight!" Small Knight said to Tiny Bear.

"I don't want to wait in the tower.

I want to be the one to save me."

"Then we shall have to do something about this monster,"

Tiny Bear squeaked. "But how?"

Small Knight and Tiny Bear studied all the maps

and read all the books in the castle, but

they couldn't find anything about the monster!

So they decided to go on a journey instead.

First, they went to the Ancient Library to speak with

the Wise Owl, who knew all that was ever written.

"I know nothing of that," the Wise Owl said.

"Have you asked the Big Bear, master of the forest?"

"I've never heard of that," the Big Bear said.

"Talk to the Queen of Moths. She knows all the spirits."

"I can't help you, little travelers," the Queen of Moths said,

"for I know nothing about the monster."

But the youngest moth flew to Small Knight and whispered:

"The Dragon hoards all the secrets.

Maybe a gift would convince him to help?"

"What do you bring the Dragon

who has everything?" Tiny Bear said.

"I don't know!" Small Knight sighed.

"What would you want, Tiny Bear?"

He thought for a bit. "Cookies! Everyone loves cookies!"

"Hello, little travelers," the Dragon said.

"What brought you here?

And what is this marvelous smell?"

"Hello, Mr. Dragon, sir," Small Knight said politely.

"We came to seek your advice.

Would you like to try a couple of cookies?"

"Maybe a couple, but only if you join me for tea!"

And so Small Knight and Tiny Bear joined the

Dragon for tea and told him their story.

The Dragon said, "No matter how far you go,

or how fast you run, you won't find what you seek.

What you should do is look inside yourself."

Small Knight and Tiny Bear thanked the all-knowing

Dragon and started sadly toward home.

What did the Dragon's advice even mean?

The monster was still there, and Small Knight could

feel it growing. Looking at the castle in the distance,

Small Knight remembered the dreadful princess lessons,

and puffy dresses, and curtsies, and waltzing, and

upsetting their parents, and being unsure and scared.

The monster felt it all—no, the monster WAS it all!

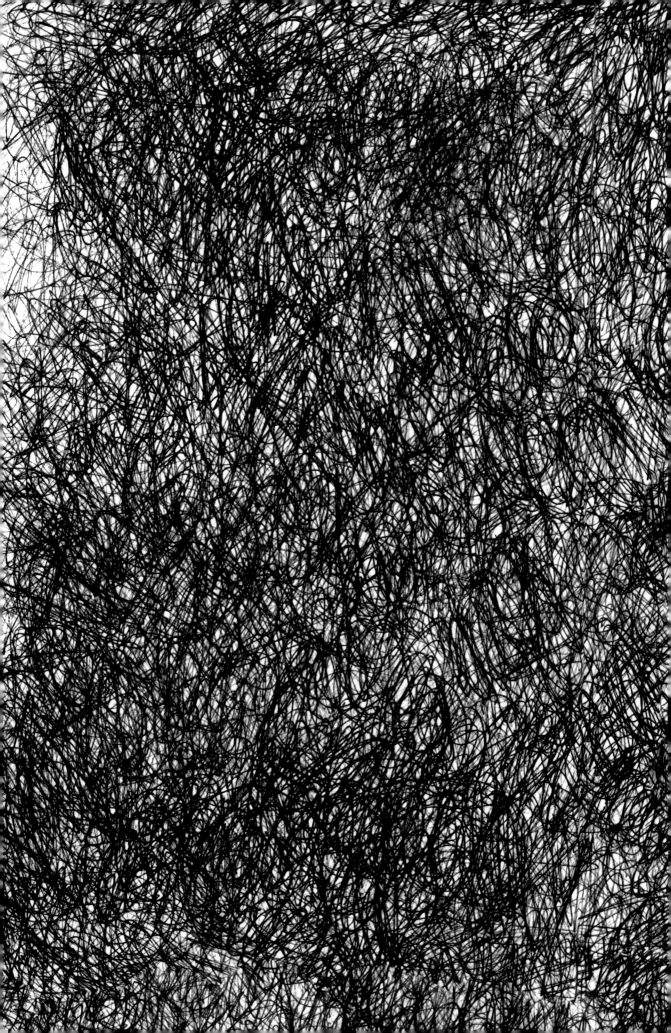

And even though Small Knight was still really scared,

they turned around and looked

the monster right in the face.

"I see you," Small Knight said.

"I know you and I know you are real.

And I am not afraid anymore."

The monster screeched, and started shrinking.

"I see you, Anxiety Monster," Small Knight repeated, more

certain now. "And I won't run away from you anymore."

The monster was hissing and twisting,

getting smaller and smaller. Soon it was just a little

spiky ball of smoke, jumping around.

"Quick!" Small Knight yelled. "Let's trap it!"

Tiny Bear grabbed an empty jug and, together with

Small Knight, shoved the hissing monster into it.

"Is that it? Did we win?" Tiny Bear asked,

looking at the jug filled with a cloudy something.

"I think so," Small Knight said.

"So, what do we do now?" Tiny Bear wondered.

"What if it grows again?"

"We take it with us," Small Knight said,

"and keep an eye on it. That way, we won't have to

keep waiting for it to reappear."

"Now let's go, Tiny Bear!" Small Knight smiled.

"We really need to be home before dinner,

so Mom and Dad don't worry!

We wouldn't want them to get

anxiety monsters of their own, would we?"

Author's Note

Facing something you are really afraid of takes a lot of courage.
Especially if facing the monster means looking inside yourself first.
And even though sometimes the monster doesn't go away for good,
Small Knight knew what to do. They were ready to face it and
tame it and keep it under control. After all, they were lucky to have
their best friend by their side. And most importantly,
they were their own very brave Small Knight.

A Feiwel and Friends Book
An imprint of Macmillan Publishing Group, LLC
120 Broadway, New York, NY 10271
mackids.com

Our books may be purchased in bulk for promotional, educational, or business use.
Please contact your local bookseller or the Macmillan Corporate and
Premium Sales Department at (800) 221-7945 ext. 5442 or by email
at MacmillanSpecialMarkets@macmillan.com.

Library of Congress Cataloging-in-Publication Data

Names: Kasha, Manka, author, illustrator.
Title: Small Knight and the Anxiety Monster / Manka Kasha.
Description: First edition. | New York : Feiwel & Friends, 2021. | Summary:
Small Knight would rather go on adventures with their best friend,
Tiny Bear, than learn to be a perfect princess, but worrying
about telling their parents creates a dreadful monster.
Identifiers: LCCN 2020039224 | ISBN 9781250618795 (hardcover)
Subjects: CYAC: Knights and knighthood—Fiction. | Princesses—Fiction. |
Sex role—Fiction. | Monsters—Fiction. | Anxiety—Fiction.
Classification: LCC PZ7.1.K37114 Sm 2021 | DDC [E]—dc23
LC record available at https://lccn.loc.gov/2020039224

First edition, 2021
Book design by Rich Deas and Kathleen Breitenfeld
The art was created with watercolor and ink.
Feiwel and Friends logo designed by Filomena Tuosto
Printed in China by RR Donnelley Asia Printing Solutions Ltd.,
Dongguan City, Guangdong Province

ISBN 978-1-250-61879-5 (hardcover)
1 3 5 7 9 10 8 6 4 2